MY BELOVED ANGEL

A Soldier's Love Story

R. Annan

One Vision Publishing

My Beloved Angel
Copyright 2014 by R. Annan
WGA Reg. # R31101 (09/29/2014)

Copy Editor: Karren Doll Tolliver
Author's Portrait by Hazel Tertsakian
Cover Artist: R. Annan

One Vision Publishing
Florida, USA
Published 2017
ISBN: 978-1-942338-62-8 (eBook)
ISBN: 978-1-942338-61-1 (Print)

Dedicated to the memory of

Elke Maria Annan

10.12.42 - 02.02.13

She was a joy to behold.

Her smile made the sun shine.

Her laughter was a soft symphony.

Her name was Elke and I will always love her.

Chapters

Cutting Ties

All roads lead to Elke and the cookie dough. In a zigzagging path across thousands of miles, first one way then another, I finally ended up where fate had me destined to be. This strange and exciting journey would have never come about had my father and I not had a disagreeable encounter one day when I was young. It took place during a heated argument and I can still remember his angry words and my defiant reply.

"John Brandon, you will do as I tell you!"

"No, Father, I won't!"

"What did you say?"

"I said no, Father, I won't do as you say!"

My answer infuriated my father and, without warning, he struck me.

My father owned a small paper box factory by the Hudson River in mid-state New York. His intentions were for me to stay at home and learn the business while my older brother and sister went on to law school. I, however, having a stubborn and rebellious nature, had ideas of my own. My preference was to either be a Wall Street broker or a card dealer in Las Vegas.

I know this sounds strange but I was always good at cards, even at an early age. My father scoffed at me and denigrated my efforts, but it was a natural skill that would serve me well all through my lifetime.

In an act of youthful rebellion, because my father had struck me, I enlisted in the Army at the age of nineteen. This was during the Korean War and it caused my mother considerable distress. But it was too late to turn back and from that moment on it seemed as if a higher power was pulling the strings and calling the shots. I felt as if I was on an endless rollercoaster with no way of getting off.

As a result of signing up for the service, I was forced to endure six months of basic training at a remote place called Indiantown Gap, in the remote hills of Pennsylvania. That meant suffering extremely long days of firing military weapons, sleeping in the field and going on twenty-mile marches with a forty-pound backpack. I hated every moment and was soon cursing myself for enlisting. As a rule I disliked hard work of any kind. I was hoping to find a desk job doing paperwork, with afternoons off to play cards or go to a restaurant and a movie.

By the time the training was over, however, my body had been transformed from sponge to rock. Whereas I had been in poor physical condition going in, I emerged from the ordeal lean and muscular and feeling very proud of myself for having survived at all. It also taught me the value of cooperation and companionship, something I had avoided as a young man..

After a month's leave at home, during which time my father and I hardly spoke to each other, I reported to a military depot in California. I still had hopes of getting a nice, easy desk job but, to my disappointment, I was quickly shipped off to South Korea on an overly crowded troop ship. I and many other fellow recruits suffered seasickness and diarrhea from the Pacific Ocean all the way to the Yellow Sea. It was a horrible, if not nauseating and smelly, experience.

After more than two weeks on rough seas, we arrived at our destination at Inchon Harbor, South Korea. It was a dark night in June when, hanging onto our duffel bags and rifles, we were loaded like sardines into landing boats and sent bouncing across the choppy water into the harbor. It was a long, bruising trip.

A train was waiting for us some hundred yards west of the harbor. As we scrambled onboard, we were handed a combat meal, a clip of ammunition for our M-1 rifles and told to be on the alert for a crazy North Korean called "Bed-Check Charley" who flew around dropping mortar rounds from his old, bi-winged airplane. Luckily for us, Charley was busy somewhere else that night.

It was still dark when our train stopped hours later. A sergeant wearing a forty-five pistol came walking down the aisle stomping his feet loudly to wake us up.

"Alright, men, grab yer c - - ks an' pull up yer socks. It's time ta move out," he yelled loudly with a Texas cowboy twang.

We quickly scrambled from the train onto a flat, open area in the middle of nowhere. A higher-ranking sergeant with a clip board yelled out our names. "Anderson, Arbuckle...Barns, Brandon, Buckley…"

As our names were called, we double-timed it over to a line of trucks, climbed in and waited. When the last soldier got on, we were driven away without so much as a word of explanation. We traveled along in the black of night on a bumpy road for what seemed hours. Eventually, we heard and saw the thunder and flash of artillery in the distance. That was where the war was going on and we were headed in its direction. A cold fear crept into my bones. I felt afraid and from the looks on the faces of my companions, they did, too.

As the sun came up on a hot, humid morning, we arrived at the bottom of a series of high hills that ran east and west as far as the eye could see. They were bare of growth, except for a few bent over scrub oaks and weeds. Roads and foot trails led up and down their slopes and there were some craters here and there made by artillery shells. Those big holes got our attention because they were made by the North Korean artillery.

We climbed out of the trucks, assembled and waited as another sergeant called out our names again. The trucks left and we were marched to a regimental holding center at the base of a hill where we were fed a hot meal. Tents and cots also awaited us there and we were given time to rest up.

After two day's rest and orientation, about two dozen of us were marched off to a replacement center in an infantry battalion a mile away. The battalion, we learned, had recently taken part in an attack on a place called Pork Chop Hill. The NKPA, the North Korean People's Army, had beat back the attack and the companies of the battalion had suffered high casualties. I and the other soldiers, were the new, raw, green replacements.

The day after we arrived, we came under heavy mortar fire. Scrambling out of our tents, we spent all that day and night in slip-trenches shaking like a leaf and eating cold C-rations. It was our first baptism of fire and put us on pins and needles. But there was worse to come.

After three days at battalion, I was assigned to a rifle company with several others. A few days later the company formed up early in the morning and marched to a staging area. Other units were already there, waiting. We had no idea what was going on until a rumor spread through the ranks. The rumor quickly proved to be true. We were going to mount an attack on Pork Chop Hill and try to retake it from the North Koreans.

Even from a mile away, bare-boned and barren, Pork Chop Hill loomed skyward completely void of vegetation. Torn apart by thousands of artillery rounds and bombs, it looked like some huge, ominous burial mound. The sight of it turned my blood cold.

We stood in platoon formation behind a rise not far from the hill, clinging to our M-1 Rifles and waiting to hear the word to attack. The soldier next to me vomited. He had swallowed too many salt pills and gotten an adverse reaction.

A nondenominational pastor came and held services for those who felt the need for spiritual support. He walked among us uttering benedictions. A few soldiers knelt to be blessed by the touch of his hand on their heads.

A warrant officer from our company walked over to where I and several other privates stood huddled together. He asked us, "Are you the new ones?"

"Yes, sir," we muttered in unison.

"When it starts, stay with me," he said. "Understand?"

We nodded. His hands shook as he lit a cigarette. It was later rumored he had orders to shoot any of us who turned and ran in the face of the enemy.

We stood there fully armed with our backpacks and helmets on and began to sweat as the hot Korean sun came up above our heads. By then, we had lost the element of surprise. They hadn't gotten us into position quietly and quickly enough for a surprise attack. Somebody had screwed up.

Luckily, at the last moment, someone from regimental or division headquarters realized our situation and sent the order to stand down. We most likely would have been slaughtered trying to take that hill again. I'm sure the NKPA had seen us getting into position and were waiting for us to attack.

We turned around and went back to our positions on the trench line, leaving the retaking of Pork Chop Hill for another day. It was said that almost a thousand NKPA were dug into the hill and waiting for us. If that were true, we most certainly would have been annihilated.

In the passing days, my company often changed positions on the trench line in an effort to keep the NKPA from guessing where we were. Myself and private, Ed Holmes, were assigned as a two-man crew on a jeep mounted 50-caliber machine gun. Our job was to provide harassing fire at night to keep the enemy off balance. Holmes was the driver and I was the gunner.

One night, when we didn't move fast enough, we caught return mortar fire and narrowly escaped. We got hit with a few small pieces of shrapnel but were not seriously wounded. After that incident, we learned to move faster and never fire from the same spot twice. The North Koreans were watching us as much as we were watching them.

On the same day that Holmes and I were promoted to Private First Class, battalion got a call from regimental headquarters informing us that the North Koreans were planning to launch an all-out attack against our area of responsibility. We were put on full alert. Everyone, including cooks, clerks, and medics, were ordered to man the trench lines and be prepared to meet the enemy head on.

Holmes, and I were instructed to park the jeep on a rise behind our company with a clear view of the battlefield. From our position, we could see past the trenches to the valley floor below. We waited anxiously in anticipation of the coming battle, staring down and looking for movement. Regiment sent up parachute flares to illuminate the landscape.

The night dragged on. A few hours before dawn, a carpet of dense fog covered the entire area. Time passed slowly. Cold and dampness set in. I had the strange feeling of being watched. Nothing moved on either side of the valley. There were hardly any sounds, only an eerie calm as we waited for something to happen. Several times Holmes and I almost dozed off.

Land of War and Frogs

Just before dawn, something did happen. We heard the distant sound of bugles coming from the far side of the valley. It grew louder and the North Korean soldiers seemed to spring up out of the earth. They came at us in waves across a five-mile section of the valley floor, each wave carrying its own red and blue battle flags. Their mortar crews gave them covering fire as they ran shooting their AK-47s up at our men in the trenches. The waves of NKPA resembled a pale-blue ocean as they rushed across the valley floor towards us.

In no time at all, they were about a hundred yards from our barbed wire. We could almost see their faces in the light of the flares. A few of them, faster than the rest, jumped the wire and ran up the long slope into our minefields. They were either blown to bits or cut down by rifle fire.

In response, Regiment sent up a massive number of parachute flares, so many that the night turned into day. I heard the boom of artillery behind us as our 155mm batteries went into action. Artillery rounds came whistling over our heads and seconds later the floor of the valley split open. Huge showers of earth shot up toward the sky. Our own mortar squad began firing 60mms down the long slope past the minefields into the rice paddies below. The riflemen sighted in and fired their M-1 rifles down from the trench line. That was our cue to go into action.

As their heavy mortar rounds burst all about us, I chambered the first round into the big 50-caliber machine gun, grabbed the dual handles and pressed my thumbs on the trigger pads. The big gun barked and bucked and the jeep shook as a stream of bullets burst from the barrel. Holmes handled the linked ammunition, letting it feed smoothly into the breech block. Standing behind the big gun. I swung it from left to right on its mount, sending an arc of bullets showering down into the valley. When the ammo can emptied out, I opened the breech and Holmes fed in a new line. We worked well together. By the time we had gone through our fifth can of ammo, the gun barrel began to smoke and I could feel the heat.

It was necessary to change the barrel. If it wasn't changed, the gun would start firing on automatic and I would have no control. It would be like trying to hold down a bucking bronco.

I got out the special gloves and wrench and then went to work unscrewing the barrel. At first it was wedged solid and wouldn't budge. It took both Ed and me to get it broke loose. What with all the action and noise going on around us, I got a little careless. As I unscrewed the hot barrel and pulled it out of the block, I swung it up on my shoulder. I felt the heat against my neck and the smell of my flak jacket being singed. In a panic, I let the hot barrel roll down over my shoulder onto the floor of the jeep.

I knew I was badly burnt because I could feel the pain and smell the seared flesh, but I chose to ignore it. This was no time to break down. Holmes and I finally got the new barrel in place and went to work again. I kept firing until the sun broke over the hills from the east. By then, the flares had stopped going up and the artillery had all but ceased.

Homes and I got a good look at what was once a blanket of green rice paddies and grass below.

I had expected to see dead bodies scattered all about, but there was nothing like that there. The surviving North Korean had taken their dead and wounded with them. All that remained on the valley floor were huge, deep holes and bare, blackened earth. An old farmer's hut that once stood there had been pounded into rubble.

The valley didn't look the same anymore. A once living, vibrant piece of earth had been ripped, gutted and smashed into mud. God's green earth had been the loser that day. We had destroyed nature in a matter of a few hours. It would take years to heal.

As for my self-inflicted wound, it wasn't bad enough to keep me off the trench line, but I did carry a large scar for over a dozen years as a reminder of my first combat in a faraway land, thousands of miles from home.

Everyone on the trench line that night was awarded the Combat Infantryman Badge. My company suffered five killed and nine wounded.

A few months later, and to our delight, the Korean War began winding down. The North Korean People's Army and the U.N. Coalition Forces were now dug in along the 38th parallel, facing each other along a complicated network of trench lines while peace-talk feelers were being put out. It now turned into a war of patrols and skirmishes, which were dangerous enough because both sides had put out minefields in the rice paddies.

Holmes and I were eventually taken off the jeep and put in a rifle squad. Every few days we snuck out into the rice paddies looking for North Korean patrols. When we did find them, it got very messy. Both sides took casualties. Holmes was wounded and sent home. I lost many more friends and had several close calls myself. I hated those patrols. We called them "bait patrols" because we were the bait to expose the enemy so battalion could call artillery in on them. Sometimes artillery got their coordinates wrong and we found ourselves running for our lives to avoid getting blown to bits. On those occasions, I suspect the North Koreans had a good laugh at us.

There were artillery battles almost every day and night, but no major frontal attacks. Eventually even the artillery battles and foot patrols stopped as the cease-fire talks finally took place.

From then on, it became a battle with the extremes of nature. The Korean winters were damp and cold. For us, it meant long, freezing hours waiting for word that the conflict was over. We slept in bunkers dug into the hillsides and ate

C-rations. Some of us got packages from home. We read the army newspaper, the Stars and Stripes.

Battalion managed to get us a hot meal, usually breakfast, once a day. But to get it you had to trek over the reverse side of the hill down to a flat area far below. Few of us had the energy to do that. Frostbite was common, especially when we came down from the trench line to lower areas where we had to sleep on the bare ground.

In the summer, we battled heat, malaria and hemorrhagic fever, a sickness spread by mosquitoes. A nasty infection, it causes high fever, internal bleeding, shock and death. To prevent malaria, we took a big, yellow pill once a week. It tasted bitter and made most of us sick to our stomachs. We called it the horse pill. It turned the whites of our eyes yellow.

During the rainy period, which was brief but intense, the dampness rotted everything. Rifles rusted in a day. Skin felt clammy and wet. It was a common thing to have the trenches fill up with six inches of water and become muddy. After a heavy downpour, thousands of small, brown frogs came crawling out of the earth. They filled the trenches and made their way down into the bunkers. To get rid of them, we had to shovel them over the lower side of the trench line. They made a squealing sound as we tossed them flying down the slope.

Frogs were around in the dry season as well. They hid in the scrub oaks, waited until you walked by and then jumped on you. It seemed like they always aimed for the mouth, eyes, ears or neck. They stuck like glue.

I was anxious for the time to come when I could leave this strange, surreal land. In the front lines, we had a different perspective than those stationed at desk jobs in the rear. For us a day seemed like a week and a week seemed like a month. A year felt like eternity.

When that day came, I could hardly believe it was real. I finally received my orders to go home to the land of baseball, hot dogs, ice cream, French fries and beer. I was happy but at the same time I was sad.

It was hard for me to say goodbye to men who had become my brothers in battle. Without digressing or dwelling on the gruesome details of battle, it is enough to say that time and time again, we cheated death by a narrow margin. Some of us had been more afraid than others, but all of us will forever carry that fear buried deep down inside us. We saw our comrades fall or be wounded in battle, but if time is a healer then, hopefully, the pain of these memories will gradually fade away.

We made promises to meet again someday, promises many of us knew we would never keep. We said it to make the parting less painful. In the trenches, we bonded together. Back in the world, distance and time would pull us apart. In the end, all we would have would be fond memories and some old, faded, wrinkled, coffee-stained photographs.

The day before I left Korea, my unit was located near Hill 347. It was somewhere between White Horse and T-Bone Hills, along the 38th parallel, south of the Demilitarized Zone. To the north, about a mile away, was the much cursed and often fought over Pork Chop Hill. It looked as bleak and ominous as ever. I was glad to put it behind me.

I was shipped back home to an engineer battalion in Fort Knox, Kentucky. I was all in one piece except for frostbite on one little toe and a burn scar on my right shoulder. It felt good to be home again.

I spent a year in Kentucky and during my time there I went back to my favorite pass time playing cards. Often, it was for money. I was good at it and, whenever I played, I mostly managed to win. My other interest was in the stock market. In high school I was a business major, so I naturally took a keen interest in what was happening on the New York Stock Exchange. I studied the best brokerage firms and chose one. Every chance I got, I sent money back to my mother, either by registered mail or travelers checks. She put it in the bank for me.

I wrote to my mother often and she answered regularly, but I never got mail from my father and only irregularly from my brother and sister. Eventually that became the norm for the rest of my life.

I managed to keep my hands clean. Literally, I mean. Through an army friend, I got a desk job in my Kentucky unit at Battalion S-3. I assisted in making out training and work schedules for the lower companies. It was that sweet job pushing paper that I had always wanted.

There wasn't much to do after work. There was always a card game going on somewhere in the battalion. On weekends, most of the single men went off base to get drunk or look for girls. Although southern girls were very amiable, they didn't take us soldiers very seriously and treated us more as a curiosity and source of information than anything else. They asked a lot of question but didn't care to talk much about themselves. They knew we were but a passing fancy on our way to distant lands. Others would come in our place.

In truth, we were all waiting to be sent to other places. The army never let you dally in one place for too long. By the end of my second year in Kentucky, I was handed orders for Europe.

I had no idea at the time, but this would be the move that fate had planned for me all along. The cookie dough was waiting for me and so was the most beautiful girl in the world.

Road to Meerholz

In 1958, at the age of twenty one, I was reassigned from Fort Knox, Kentucky to a place called Hanau, in central Germany. My new unit, an engineer battalion, was housed in a *Kaserne*, or German barracks, which had once been occupied by a German tank battalion but was now leased to the American Army. It had a fuel depot, a motor park and a maintenance shop. The Army added a PX, a commissary, a barber shop and a medical unit. There was also a money exchange kiosk near the gate. As luck would have it, I was again assigned to Battalion S-3 doing the same job as at my previous unit. By now I had attained the rank of corporal. The gambling with cards continued.

Army life in Germany was mostly routine. You worked from Monday until Friday afternoon. From Friday evenings until midnight Sunday night, if you had no other duty, you were on your own to go into town and get drunk, chase German girls, or both. Mostly it was chasing German girls. But for me, it was pretty much just playing cards although I did visit a few bars in Hanau and get in a few dances between drinks. But buying drinks for bar girls got old very quick and paid no dividends. You left drunk and empty handed.

One Saturday morning I was in the barracks, lying on my cot after a long night at poker. I had intended to sleep until around noon then go over to the Post Exchange snack bar and eat. After that, I would go into town. Suddenly I felt someone kicking my cot.

"Hey! New York! Wake up!" I rubbed my eyes and sat up. It was Private Larsen, a young soldier from Texas who worked in the motor pool.

"Okay, Larsen," I said. "Knock it off, you jerk!"

"You wiped me out last night, Brandon," he said. "I'm as busted as a broke-back mule." Larsen was known for his down to earth vocabulary.

"You don't play cards very well, Larsen," I replied. "Maybe you should try knitting."

"Yeah, I might just do that," he replied. He looked a bit lost.

"So, what do you want?"

"How about loaning me ten for gas, so I can drive up to Meerholz," he said.

"Where the heck is Meerholz?"

"About twenty clicks north of Hanau," Larsen replied. A click is a kilometer, a short mile.

"So, what's up in Meerholz?"

"A graduation party. I'm supposed to meet my girl there."

"College?" I asked.

"No, high school," he said.

I laughed. "I bet her folks don't know she's messing around with a G.I., do they?"

"Hell, no. And her dad's a cop, too!"

"Yeah? Well, I hope he nails your Texas butt to the barn," I said.

We both laughed. Suddenly I felt like I'd had enough of playing cards for a while. The party in Meerholz sounded like a lot of fun.

"I hear the Germans really know how to throw a good party," I said.

Larsen didn't say anything. He was probably thinking that I wanted an invitation to go along. I knew he thought I was one of those dumb Yankees from New York. But, at the same time he needed the money and his friends were too broke to lend him any.

I gave him an opening. "You want some company on the drive up there?"

He mulled that over, but I already knew the answer. "Ah, well, no, not really."

He looked away toward the other cots. They were all empty except for two soldiers at the far end who were still asleep. Since it was a Saturday, almost everyone was still in Hanau.

"Is it by invitation only?" I asked.

"Yeah, something like that."

"Yeah? Well, you're full of crap," I said.

I jumped up, pushed Larsen aside, grabbed my toilet articles and towel from my locker, locked it and headed for the latrine. He called me a few choice names as I walked away. When I finally came back, he was gone. Getting dressed in my civilian clothes, I left the barracks and walked slowly over to the snack bar to get a bite to eat.

About an hour later, as I walked toward the gate to take a taxi into Hanau, Larsen drove up alongside me in his old, beat up German four door sedan. He honked the horn and stopped. "Come on! Get in!"

I got in and handed him a ten-dollar bill. He filled up at the base gas station and we headed out for Meerholz.

Once outside of Hanau, Larsen pulled onto a narrow country road that wound northeast past green pastures and lush farmlands. Above us was a deep blue sky marked with a few puffy white clouds. Through the open window I could smell the pungent odor of growing things. I inhaled and felt invigorated. The air smelled fresh and clean. Suddenly, Germany was just great. It felt good to be outside the walls of the compound.

It's a good day for a party, I thought. I felt good. I hadn't been outside much, what with playing cards and all. "What's her name?" I asked, looking at Larsen. "Your girlfriend?"

"Frieda."

I laughed. "They're all named Frieda."

"It's as common as your stupid name, Brandon!"

"Yeah? Well, how do you like being called 'parson', huh, Larsen?"

The conversation went like that while we drove on, passing through the town of Rodenbach. We kept going until we finally came into the small village of Meerholz. Larsen drove slowly until we saw a large, two-story house where a bunch of kids were milling around in small groups, going in and out, chatting and yelling in German. Some were singing but most of them were drinking from bottles or steins. A few were stuffing food into their mouths.

Larsen parked behind another car. We got out and walked over to the house, making our way past a girl who was throwing up while her boyfriend held her purse. Just getting in the door was a chore by itself. Once inside, we went looking for Larsen's girlfriend. Wandering around the bottom floor, we squeezed between bodies that jerked about. Arms flailed without warning making us duck and swerve to avoid getting a black eye, a smashed lip or a broken nose.

We struggled from one room to the other with no success, and then started up the stairs to the second floor, getting our heads butted and our bellies punched. Sometimes we ended up accidently stepping on someone's hands or feet. The strange part of it was no one seemed to notice or care.

At last, we made it to the top. It was here, in a large, mostly bare room with bookshelves along its walls, where we found Larsen's Frieda. She was not alone. Another girl was with her. Larsen introduced me to Frieda, and Frieda introduced me to the girl.

"This is Elke," Frieda said to me in very clear English.

"Oh, hello, Jawn," this girl named Elke said, pronouncing my name as 'Jawn' instead of John. She spoke American with sort of an English accent.

I looked down at her and was stunned. For a moment, I thought I must be dreaming. She was the most beautiful creature I had ever seen in all my life.

Cookie Dough

This little dream of a girl and I stood staring at each other as if we were the only two people in the room. She looked up at me and I looked down at her gorgeous face. Oh God, what a face it was! I was totally hypnotized. Her short, dark-brown hair barely reached down to her delicate neck. Her unblemished forehead and cheeks were exquisitely sculpted and her symmetrical nose and gull-wing mouth, above a gently rounded chin, were perfect. Her gray-blue eyes stared into mine, penetrating deep into my soul.

Suddenly I realized that we were alone. Larsen and Frieda had snuck off to a far corner of the room to be by themselves. I caught a glimpse of them kissing, but mostly I kept staring at this incredible girl in front of me.

"Why are you staring at me, Jawn?" Her voice had a musical lilt to it. The way she said my name made me want to hear her say it again and again, "Jawn! Jawn! Jawn!" I was totally speechless. She said, "Why don't we find a chair and sit down?"

Quickly snapping out of it, I replied, "Okay, sure. Let's do that."

She grabbed me by the hand and pulled me along as if I were a little boy. Oh, I would have followed her anywhere, anywhere at all. Just put a leash around my neck.

After looking around, we found an old chair with a bent back and no arms. "Please sit down, Jawn," she said.

I acted the gentleman and said, "No, please, you first."

"Oh, no, you. You must sit down first," she insisted. "Then I will sit down."

I was a bit confused but decided to do what she asked. I would have done anything for her. You want me to shoot myself in the head? Okay, I can do that. Anything else you want, just tell me and I'll be glad do it, no matter what it is.

I carefully took my place on the rickety old chair. She waited until I had settled in place, then turned around and tossed her dress up in back. I was pleasantly surprised but had no time to fully enjoy the sight because she quickly sat down on my lap. The chair groaned and tilted. I braced for a fall but, to my relief and surprise, the old thing didn't break apart.

"I hope it can hold us!" Elke said, laughing. She took my hand and placed it around her slim waist. "Don't let me fall, Jawn!" As if I ever would.

"You speak very good English," I said. "Did you go to school in England?"

"Oh, no! Miss Sturbridge came over from London to teach at my school," she explained.

"I'd say she was a good teacher."

"Oh, yes. Very good."

I glanced at the bookshelves. "There are a lot of books here."

"A teacher lives here," she said. "Do you read much?"

"No, not so much. Mostly the newspapers," I replied.

"I just finished reading *A Farewell to Arms*," she said. "The woman died in the end, and the man cried terribly. Would you cry for me, if you loved me and I was dying, Jawn?"

I stared at her thinking it was an odd thing to say but somehow her words seemed deeply moving. I didn't know how to reply, so I said, "You're not planning to die soon, are you?"

She laughed and then smiled. "Oh, gosh no, I hope not."

"Have you read any of the books here?" I asked.

"Oh, yes. Lots of them. Many are written in English."

"I see," I said.

"You see what?"

"That many are written in English and that a teacher lives here."

Suddenly she laughed. The chair started to sway and groan, then stopped and held again.

"What's so funny?" I asked.

"You and I are funny," she said.

"Oh? Why is that?"

"Because we are sitting in an old chair that is going to break and we are making small talk!"

"And that's funny?" I asked.

"It certainly could be, if the chair breaks!"

Suddenly she hopped off my lap, grabbed one of my hands and gave it a tug.

"Come on," she said. "I want to show you a trick."

She led me away and the chair fell over with a bang. We went to the stairs. It was rough going because of the crowd, but after a struggle, we made it down to the bottom floor where we stood facing each other, staring into each other's eyes.

She smiled, as if in delicious anticipation of a coming event. "Come, Jawn," she said innocently but with a mischievous fire in those lovely eyes.

She pulled me through a doorway into another room that I quickly recognized as a kitchen. An elderly woman in a blue dress and a white apron was working in front of a big, iron stove. I caught the smell of something baking in the oven. Nearby, I noticed several stools. A tray of freshly made cookie dough was on each stool, waiting for its turn in the oven. I was staring at them when Elke spoke to me.

"Do you like cookies, Jawn?" she asked, standing directly behind me.

I turned around to answer. "Yes, I do, very much."

"Are you sure?"

"Yes," I said, "I'm sure."

"Then, do have some, Jawn!" she said, trying to hold back a giggle. At that moment, she shoved me backwards!

The old woman screamed. She reached out to catch me but was too late. Falling backwards, I ended up sitting squarely on the nearest tray of soft, gooey cookie dough. I immediately jumped up but the damage was done. I can't describe the feeling of embarrassment and surprise that came over me as I stood there weighting several pounds heavier in the rear.

As for my little pixie, she was nowhere to be seen.

Bumstead Sandwich

So, there I stood in the kitchen in a house in the village of Meerholz, Germany, with long strands of cookie dough hanging from the seat of my pants. The cute, little darling who pushed me into it had run off and left me alone to fend for myself.

The woman who had tried to save me began to laugh. Her high-pitched, hysterical caterwauling first got the attention of a few curious partygoers, then more and more. Quite suddenly, I became the center of attention, and within seconds a large throng of onlookers had gathered to see the freak show. The laughter started as a trickle, then quickly became a roar as a crowd came down from upstairs to see what the fuss was all about.

"Verrückter Amerikaner!" someone yelled. Fingers pointed in my direction.

"Idiot! Dummkopf!"

I wondered where Elke had gone and why Larsen and Frieda weren't there to help me. I was trapped. There was no way I could make my way through that mocking crowd.

Suddenly, the woman came over, waved a hand at them. and shouted, "*Raus!*" That did it. They all scattered. She turned to me and said, "Come!"

I followed her through a door into an adjoining room, which turned out to be a laundry room. She gave me a towel, made some charade-like gestures, then turned her back while I removed my trousers and wrapped the towel around my waist. As soon as I was finished, she grabbed my pants and emptied the contents of the pockets into a large bowl.

"Go!" she growled, pointing through the doorway. "*Essen!*" I got her meaning and quickly went into the kitchen.

I found a large table there stacked high with all kinds of food. There were loaves of sliced farmer's bread, pots of pickles, jars of mayonnaise, mustard and relish and platters of blood sausage, liverwurst, ham, salami and other cold cuts. There were also heads of lettuce, tomatoes and onions. In this mix were also piles of cookies and cakes and pastries of every kind.

Next to the table was a large tub of iced beer, apple wine and citrus water. A lot of this food I had never seen before.

Have you ever heard of a Dagwood Bumstead Sandwich? Well, it's a large sandwich stacked high with cold cuts, mayonnaise, mustard, onions, tomatoes, pickles and lettuce between two slices of bread. I made a beautiful Dagwood Bumstead sandwich, grabbed a bottle of beer and sat down on a chair to have a feast. A few people came by, laughing at the crazy American, but I ignored them.

I had just finished eating when Frieda and Larsen came in through the crowd. That little pixie, Elke, was hiding behind them, trying not to be seen. She held her hands over her mouth in an effort to stop giggling.

"What happened?" Larsen asked, trying to keep a straight face.

"Oh, nothing," I answered.

"They said some drunken American had sat down in a tray of cookie dough," Frieda said.

"Was that you?" Larsen taunted. He could very well see it was me and was enjoying the moment.

"Nope. Some other guy," I said.

"Well, where are your trousers?" Frieda asked.

"The cook has them," I replied.

Larsen gloated. "Pal, if this ever gets back to the guys in the barracks, they'll all be calling you 'the little dough boy'," he taunted.

"Who cares," I growled. "At least I got a free meal and a beer out of it."

Frieda pulled Elke out in front to face me. "She wants to apologize," Frieda said. "She told me what happened."

Elke gave me a sad look that we both knew was phony.

"What for?" I said. "She didn't do anything. I got stupid and sat down on the wrong chair, that's all." I stood up and smiled at Elke. "Isn't that right?"

"Why yes, that is right. Jawn got stupid," Elke said. Then she giggled and said, "All Americans are stupid!"

"Elke!" Frieda was surprised and angry. She jerked Elke's arm.

"No, no," I said quickly, looking at Larsen. "She's right. All Americans are stupid."

"Well, perhaps not all of them," Elke corrected. "Maybe just you."

"Sure, just me."

She giggled again and looked at me. "You really are stupid, Jawn. You agree with everything I say about you!"

Larsen said, "You two love birds go ahead and argue. We're going back upstairs."

He grabbed two bottles of beer and, with Frieda, disappeared back into the crowd.

"What are you going to do now, Jawn?" Elke said. "You have no pants."

"You stay away from me," I said.

"Why, Jawn? Don't you love me anymore?" she replied teasingly.

"Maybe, maybe not. Now scram, beat it!" I said, even though I didn't mean it.

"Alright, Jawn, if you want, I'll scram!"

Suddenly she had a very mischievous smile on her lips. Her eyes went wide, as she made a quick lunge for the towel.

I saw it coming but too late. We stood there engaged in a game of Steal the Towel. The crowd was cheering her on.

"Are you crazy?" I yelled. "Let go!"

I tried to push her hand away but lost the fight. She backed off with the towel, waving it at me as if it were a battle flag and she had won the battle. She ran into the cheering crowd.

Now it started all over again with the crowd laughing and pointing at me, as I stood there in my undershorts. I rushed back into the laundry room. The cook was finishing my pants on an ironing board. She ran a flat iron over them one last time and handed them to me. When she saw that I had lost the towel, she burst out laughing.

"*Kellah, kellah!*" she said. "*Was ist los mit du?*"

All I could do was shrug and smile. I hadn't understood a word she had said but from the look on her face, I figured she was saying that I was pathetic. I put my pants on, and then transferred my things from the bowl back into my pockets. I handed her a ten-mark bill. She grunted and pushed my hand away, refusing the money. I left, wondering if she was the wife of the owner of the house.

I walked out into the hallway and looked around, suddenly realizing that I was all alone. Larsen and Frieda had gone off somewhere to engage in their favorite pastime of kissing. The little trickster, Elke, was nowhere in sight.

I was ready to leave. This whole thing had been a bad experience as far as I was concerned. I decided to find Larsen and get out of there as quickly as possible.

That didn't work out so well.

Mad as Hell

I maneuvered through the downstairs crowd looking for Larsen and Frieda but came across that cute, little pest Elke instead. Some big German kids, probably her classmates, surrounded her. When she saw me, she held up the towel and waved it, laughing. They saw me and laughed, too. I turned my back on her and went upstairs.

After walking around in the crowd for a while, I found Larsen and Frieda in a far corner. They were kissing again and didn't see me until I snuck up and tapped Larsen on the shoulder. He jumped back, spinning round, a frightened look on his face.

When he saw that it was only me, he sighed and said, "Man, don't do that! I thought you were her old man!"

"Why? Is Frieda under age?" I asked. "And Elke, is she under age, too?"

Frieda smiled and said, "Elke likes you, John."

"What? You're kidding me, right?" I said with a scowl.

"No, no, she really likes you."

"Yeah, well, I find that hard to believe."

"No. If she didn't like you, John, she would have ignored you. Completely ignored you."

"Well, she sure as hell didn't ignore me," I said harshly, sneering.

"Did she sit on your lap?" Frieda asked.

"Yeah, so what? Is that supposed to mean something?"

"Oh, yes, it means that she really, really likes you."

I exploded: "Excuse me for saying so, but you're crazy, Frieda. You're crazy and she's crazy and you're all crazy!"

"How about me, pal?" Larsen chuckled. "Am I crazy, too?"

"Yeah, you too, pal," I said.

Frieda gave me a sad look and said, "Would you like to meet another girl, John?"

I thought for a moment. "Sure, why not?" I would get revenge on Little Miss Crazy.

"Alright," Frieda said. She went off into the crowd.

"What's the matter, Brandon, having a bad day, pal?" Larsen chuckled. It was all a big joke to him.

"Wait until we play cards again, Larsen. I'll wipe you out!"

Larsen put a friendly hand on my shoulder and smiled warmly. "Hey, look, man, this is Germany. Relax, have a good time. And don't be so serious."

I looked away and then back. I sighed. "Yeah, I suppose you're right."

"Heck, forget her! Move on, man! Get drunk! Have a ball!"

"Yeah, I just might do that."

Frieda came back. She was alone. "I'm sorry, John. All the other girls seem to be with someone."

I shrugged. "I guess they don't want to be seen with the crazy American, huh?" Elke had put a curse on me. I was now poison.

"It's not that, John," Frieda said.

"Hey, it's okay! I understand!"

"Don't be sad, John," Frieda replied.

"Go get a beer, pal," Larsen said. He looked sympathetic. "You'll feel better."

I went down to the kitchen, got a bottle of beer and stood there drinking. The old woman smiled sadly at me.

How did that little beauty twist me around so fast? How the heck did she do it? I asked myself.

I drank four beers very quickly and, by the time I went upstairs again, my legs were rubbery. I saw Elke there, standing next to Frieda and Larsen. I didn't even look at her. I just turned around, went down to the kitchen for another beer and took it out to the car. I sat there, in the dark, drinking. After a while I fell half asleep. I say half asleep because there was too much noise outside to fall asleep. I remember someone falling against the car, cursing and kicking a tire, then leaving.

Later, when things had quieted down, I had the impression that someone got quietly into the car, kissed me softly on the mouth and left. But I couldn't be sure it wasn't just a dream. After a while, I realized the car was moving and we were heading back to the *Kaserne*. I sat up and rubbed my eyes. Larsen looked over at me. For some reason, he had a big smile on his face.

"You okay, dough boy?" Larsen asked.

I yawned and asked, "What time is it?"

"Time to go home, partner," Larsen said. "Time to go home." I smiled because he had called me partner.

He hit the gas a bit harder and we sailed away into the night. Suddenly he said something I thought was a little bit strange.

"They don't mean a thing, my friend," he said, almost as if speaking to himself. "We come and we go, and they know it. You can't make the mistake of getting serious about them. It's just a game."

Later, I would understand more clearly what he meant.

Falling in Love

The next morning Larsen came and kicked my cot again. I awoke with a hangover and in a bad mood. I was still angry about the cookie dough incident. He told me he was going back to Meerholz to see Frieda. If I wanted to go, we could drive from there to Gelnhausen, where Elke lived, then drive to Frankfurt and hit the bars and restaurants.

"I'll take a pass," I said. I'd had enough of Little Miss Dough Girl. If I never saw her again it would be too soon. Anyway, the weekend wasn't over yet and I still had one last day to enjoy it.

Larsen borrowed another ten dollars and left. I went back to sleeping.

I got up about three in the afternoon, cleaned up, dressed up and took a taxi into Hanau. I walked around, stopping at the magazine kiosks and *bratwurst* vendors. Later I got hungry so I had a *Fleischwurst* with sauerkraut and mustard and a flip-top beer. I walked some more until I finally wandered into a *Kino* and watched two movies called *Das Indische Grabmal* and *Der Schinderhannes*.

When I came out it was dark. I was hungry again, so I found a restaurant near the theatre where I ordered *rouladen* with parsley-potatoes and shredded red cabbage. I washed it down with a stein of beer, and then ordered *apfelstrudel* with coffee. After that, I went to the nearest bar and got drunk. At some point, some Germans were kind enough to place me in a taxi and send me back to the *Kaserne*. I awoke the next morning with another hangover.

For the following three weeks, I avoided Larsen. Once my head cleared up I went back to playing cards. Larsen had heeded my advice and stopped gambling, so I never got the chance to clean him out again, as much as I wanted to. Since he worked in the motor pool, I didn't get to see him during the day except at the mess hall or in the barracks. Whenever we did talk, I kept our conversations as short as possible. But he always had a know-it-all smile on his face when we met and I knew why. He knew I was about to wave the white flag of surrender.

During all this time, as hard as I tried, I couldn't get that little troublemaker Elke out of my mind.

During the day at S-3, while I was plotting training and work schedules, my thoughts would drift away from my work. Her gorgeous face would pop up in my mind's eye. To make things worse, it crept into my card playing so much so that I decided to drop out for a while to get my head on straight again.

One Friday I met Larsen in the mess hall at the evening meal. We both had trays of food and were looking for a place to sit down.

"How is Frieda doing?" I asked.

"Great, just great," Larsen said. "Elke and her are working at a hair salon in Gelnhausen."

"Oh, right, no more school," I said.

"Yeah, they're out of school now," Larsen replied.

Suddenly someone called to him and he went over and sat with some buddies. I got a table nearby. Several times, as we ate, Larsen looked in my direction to see if I was still there. After a while he came over with his empty tray.

"You like to dance?" he asked.

I shrugged and said, "Sure, why?"

"Meet me in the parking lot at seven," he said. Before I could answer, he was gone.

I sat there and thought about what he had said about dancing and meeting him in the parking lot. I took that to mean he was taking Frieda dancing and wanted me along to help pay the tab. That pretty little troublemaker, Elke, would probably be there too, since she and Frieda were inseparable.

It occurred to me that this was my chance to get back at her. Once we got to a bar, I could snub her. I could leave her sitting while I danced with other German girls. The more I thought about it, the more I liked it. She had messed with the wrong American soldier. No, I wasn't going to be her patsy. I would make her very, very sorry for that little cookie dough trick. I would spoil her evening, but good.

Two hours later I was cleaned up and waiting in the parking lot. In a few minutes, Larsen came walking up to me. He was smiling and seemed very happy.

"Where are we going?" I asked.

"First to Meerholz, then Gelnhausen," he said.

"Oh?" I said dryly, pretending not to be excited.

In about a half hour, we drove into Meerholz, picked up Frieda and continued north to Gelnhausen. It was just turning evening when we got there. Larsen slowed down, drove through an alley and up a steep cobblestone street to an open area called the *Marktplatz*. He stopped in front of a four-story stone apartment house with a tile roof. Elke was standing in the doorway dressed in a simple white dress with spaghetti straps. She had on low heeled shoes.

Something strange happened to me when I saw her. She looked so beautiful that all I could think of was seeing her, hearing her voice, and being close to her again. Somehow, revenge had flown out the window. I knew then and there that I could never hurt this wonderful, gorgeous creature. I surrendered completely.

What I did next surprised not only me but also everyone else who looked on.

I got out of the car and rushed up to her. Before she could say a word, I took her in my arms and kissed her. She didn't resist so I kissed her again and again, stopping only when I realized that she was not alone. A middle-aged woman was directly behind her, in the shadows, glaring at me.

"Oh gosh, Jawn!" Elke exclaimed, catching her breath. "Gosh!" She cleared her throat and said, "Jawn, would you like to meet my mother?"

If looks could kill, at that moment I would have been dead. All I can recall is that Elke's mother growled something at me then turned around and stomped angrily into the building. I felt very, very stupid.

"What did she say?" I asked Elke.

"Oh, it's alright, Jawn," she said, giggling.

As Elke took my hand and pulled me towards the car, I could hear Frieda and Larsen laughing. Heads stuck out of the windows above, staring down at us. Elke and I got in and Larsen drove the car across the *Platz* and headed west, out of town.

I asked Frieda what Elke's mother had said to me. "Oh," Frieda said, "she said that you are a fine young man, John, and her daughter is lucky that you are interested in her." Then she, Elke and Larsen burst out into hilarious laughter.

"It's a good thing she didn't have a shotgun, Brandon," Larsen said. "She would have splattered you all over the sidewalk."

Elke smiled at me. "It's alright, Jawn. She's really nice when you get to know her."

This got Frieda and Larsen laughing once more. It was a long time before they settled down to kissing again.

On the outskirts of Frankfurt, Larsen found a bar and we went in. It was very cozy. The lights were low and couples danced to slow music. We found a table in a dark corner and ordered beer for us and soda for the girls. We drank for a while, then danced. I held her close.

"That's Nat King Cool," Elke said, referring to the music coming from the juke box. I chuckled. "Is that funny?" she asked.

"Nat King Cole," I said. "Not Nat King Cool."

I kissed her and we kept on dancing.

"Don't kiss me so much, Jawn, unless you are serious."

"Alright," I replied. I kissed her again.

"I just finished school," she said as if warning me off.

"I know," I replied and held her closer.

We stayed at the bar dancing and drinking and had a great time. I was in love and everything was wonderful. It was just us and nothing else in the world existed. I never wanted it to end. We danced and danced and I held her in my arms like a precious, fragile thing that I wanted to protect from the world, to keep her forever safe in my arms. I didn't want to share her with anyone.

The days passed quickly after that special night. The four of us became inseparable. We went on picnics in the countryside and to movies together. We visited some old castles and historical places and went swimming a few times, too. We even went fishing once, but that didn't turn out so well because of the putting of the worms on the hooks. That spooked the girls badly.

But after a while a strange thing began to happen. The closer I got to Elke and the closer Larsen got to Frieda, the farther apart we got as couples. Later, as I thought about it, it seemed a natural thing to happen. We all stayed friends, of course, especially Elke and Frieda, who had grown up together.

One day, I bought a used car. That cut the bonds between Larsen and me because it let me move about on my own, to come and go as I pleased. I brought flowers and candy to Elke's mother as a peace offering and she graciously accepted them. Elke was her only child. Her husband, Elke's father, was a young soldier when he died on the Russian Front during World War II. His body lay at rest in the Gelnhausen Cemetery.

Heartbreak

One day I heard a rumor that Larsen had received orders to return stateside. In six months he would be gone. I waited for him to say something. Weeks went by and, when he didn't tell me, I figured he had his reasons for not wanting to talk about it. Anyway, it was none of my business. It was between him and Frieda. I never mentioned it to Elke and she never told me that Frieda knew about him leaving.

His time in Germany was getting shorter each passing week. One day in the mess hall I spoke to him about it. "I heard you're getting short," I said.

He shrugged. "Yeah. So what?"

"How come you didn't tell me?"

"I was going to."

"Does Frieda know?" He looked away and shrugged. "You haven't told her, have you?"

I already knew the answer to that because, if Frieda had known, she would have told Elke and Elke would have told me.

"It's none of your business, Brandon," Larsen said. He was both embarrassed and angry. "Anyway, you wouldn't understand." After that, Larsen avoided me completely.

I should have told Elke right away what was up, but I didn't. That was because I never believed Larsen would leave Germany without saying goodbye to Frieda. I didn't think he was the kind of person who would sneak off like a rat deserting a ship and leave her hanging in the wind. So, I kept putting it off, figuring he would tell her. I had always thought that Larsen would ask Frieda to marry him. Even if he had, there just wasn't time now for all the paperwork and arrangements, even though she was now eighteen and didn't need her parents' permission.

Later, after Larsen had left for America, Elke told me a story. Frieda's father didn't like Larsen and had threatened to kill him if she married him. In a way, I saw how bad Larsen's situation was. The only solution for Larsen was to send for Frieda once he got to America but he never did. Later, Elke told me that rumors in Meerholz had it that

Frieda had an abortion a month after Larsen left. At any rate, Frieda's family moved somewhere else. Frieda never let Elke know where. She never heard from her dear friend again.

I could see the worried look on Elke's face. I guess her mother had told her that I might do the same thing to her as Larsen had done to Frieda. Sometimes, while we were sitting alone somewhere in a small, secluded bistro, I could see the tears in her eyes, even though she tried to smile and hide them. It hurt me to see that.

I knew what I wanted to do. One day I asked Elke to marry me. She said she wanted to get her mother's blessing first. I waited, thinking that her mother would put an end to us. A week went by and then, to my utter surprise, Elke told me her mother had agreed to the marriage.

Her mother insisted that we get engaged first, at least for a few months, while she posted the customary banns of the upcoming marriage in the local newspapers. During this period, through my company commander and battalion chaplain, I requested the Army's permission to marry a German citizen. It took a month to get that settled.

We got married three times in June, once in the old gothic church in Gelnhausen, once at the Gelnhausen City

Hall, and finally on the *Kaserne*, by the chaplain. By the time it was all over we felt very, very much married.

I found a small, furnished, one room efficiency on the ground floor of a home not far from the *Kaserne*. It had a foldout couch and a tiny kitchen with a small electric stove in one corner. I bought a radio from the Post Exchange and we settled down in our own little seventh heaven. The owners, an old German couple, lived above us. The rent was very reasonable. At night we would lie in bed in the dark, listen to soft music and make plans for the future.

"How many children do you want, Jawn?"

"Maybe two."

"A boy and a girl?"

"Yes," I said, "A boy and a girl."

"When we go to America, will we see the Statue of Liberty?"

"Maybe, if we go by boat. It's in New York Harbor."

"Oh, I do want to see the Statue of Liberty, Jawn. Very much. It's all green, isn't it?"

I chuckled. "Yes, it's green, just like money." We laughed.

Nights like that were very nice. Being married to her felt good. I applied for and was granted a two-week honeymoon leave. Elke and I bought sunglasses. I purchased a book of gas stamps at the Post Exchange and some soda, snacks and magazines for her to read on the road.

Leaving Germany on a sunny Saturday morning, I drove past Hanau and headed south towards Darmstadt, Mannheim, and Heidelberg. Once we were past Strasbourg, we left Germany and entered France. I sometimes drove for twelve hours at a stretch, avoiding cities and taking two-lane back roads into wine country, past vineyards and through farmlands. We skirted around Lyon and Nimes. We finally hit the Gulf of Lion and went along endless stretches of sandy beaches on our left.

We slept on the beaches in my Army pup tent. Once I sat up to act as guard but I dozed off and was awakened by a large stray dog that was licking my nose. I almost had a heart attack but Elke laughed until her sides ached. We went on to Beziers, Narbonne and Perpignan. Then it was over the Pyrenees out of France and into Spain to Figueres. From there it was another long stretch of sandy beaches along the Costa Brava to Mataro and into Barcelona where we stayed at a pension.

We saw our first bullfight in Barcelona. We didn't enjoy it at all. A horse was gored to death and a bullfighter was severely hurt. Maybe that's why they call bullfighting "death in the afternoon." The way they killed the bull was messy. We left with a bad feeling. After a week in the sun at the beach by Barcelona, we drove north to Figueres and on up through the Pyrenees mountains into France again. At that time is was easy for American soldiers to cross the borders using their I.D. cards. We spent a few days on the beach on the Costa Brava in southeastern France, and finally arrived back in Gelnhausen, sunburned and exhausted.

Elke's mother was glad to see her alive. I think she still thought of me as the crazy American who had kidnapped her only child.

Near the end of my four-year tour in Germany, Elke became pregnant. We were very excited. Elke's mother couldn't wait to become a grandmother, and she fawned over Elke every waking moment. I myself felt a certain amount of hubris. It was both terrifying and wonderful. The baby would be born just in time, just before we shipped out to Fort Devens, Massachusetts.

On a nasty, cold November night the baby announced its coming, I drove Elke to the hospital in Frankfurt. It was raining so hard I made a wrong turn, got lost and had to double back to get on the right road again. I didn't think we would make it in time but we just barely did. Elke was nearly past labor when they took her into the delivery room. The stress on her was beginning to show. Her face was pasty white and I saw the pain there. I sat in the hallway waiting. Time seemed to stand still. I finally had to get up and walk along the corridor several times.

After what seemed an eternity, a doctor and nurse came out to talk to me. I could tell by their faces that something had gone wrong. The doctor put a hand on my shoulder. He shook his head, looking very sad. "We couldn't save the baby," he said. "I'm so sorry."

"We did all we could," the nurse said.

"Is she alright?"

"She's going to be fine," the doctor said. "She will need a long rest." Then he said, "I'm sorry to tell you this, but I think she should not become pregnant again. It could pose a serious health problem."

"Can we do anything for you?" the nurse asked.

"No, thank you, but can I see her now?"

"She's heavily sedated," the doctor said. "It would be best if you waited a few hours. Let her rest."

"There's a cafeteria downstairs," the nurse said. "Perhaps you'd like some hot coffee?"

I nodded, then went down to the bottom floor to the cafeteria and got a steaming, hot cup of coffee and took it outside on the terrace to drink it in the fresh air. The rain had slacked off, but a cold wind blew in from the nearby pine trees. It felt refreshing. I stood there a while, trying to clear my head. Before long I was chilled to the bone, so I took the coffee upstairs and waited. I finished the coffee there and dozed off, only to wake up with the nurse gently shaking me. She took me in to see Elke.

"She's still a little under it," the nurse said. "So just go easy." She left us alone.

I looked down at my darling, my beloved angel. She knew it was me, but could only manage a weak smile. I leaned down and kissed her lips. I took one of her tiny, frail hands in mine. I bent and kissed it again and again. It was as cold as ice.

"I love you," I said. "I don't care about the rest of it. Nothing else matters, only you. Do you understand, my darling?" She closed her eyes and managed a weak nod. "Good. Now you have to get better. Promise me you'll get better. Please, oh, God!"

Hot, searing tears welled up in my eyes. I tried to hold them back but I couldn't. I began to cry. As I did so, she reached up a hand to touch my cheek.

"Are you crying for me, Jawn?"

"Yes, my heart, I'm crying for you."

She patted my arm to comfort me.

She began to cry, too. "He left Frieda, Jawn. You won't leave me, will you my love?"

"Never! I swear! May God strike me dead, my darling. You belong to me and I belong to you. That's how it's going to be forever, my angel! You believe me, don't you?"

"Yes, I believe you, Jawn, I believe you."

"Good, now rest, my sweet."

"Are you going away, Jawn?"

"Never, darling, never! I'll stay right here! You just rest and I'll stay right here."

She forced a smile. "The Statue of Liberty, Jawn, is it really green?"

"Yes, my love, it is sort of green, like money."

She nodded and smiled, inhaling deeply with closed eyes, falling asleep as I watched.

Separation

Not long after Elke was released from the Frankfurt hospital, we drove to Gelnhausen with a small urn that contained the baby's ashes. Elke's mother, Else, had wanted the baby to have a proper burial, so when she found out we had the baby cremated, she was very upset. I got out in front and took the blame. Else said she would have wanted the baby buried in the Gelnhausen cemetery next to her husband. I replied that Elke and I would most likely be traveling a lot and might not be coming back to Germany for a long time. I couldn't give her a better explanation, or even think of one. I felt very bad about the whole matter. Elke's mother never did fully agree and I'm sure she held it against me.

We asked Elke's mother if she wanted to come up with us to the hill above the town to release the baby's ashes. She declined, so we told her we would be back in a little while. She was on the verge of crying as we left. We drove across the *Marktplatz* to a dirt road and followed it up a steep hill to where it came to an end. It was a solemn, gusty, gray evening. The trees were bare skeletons that waved and whispered to us in the wind. We got out of the car and walked over to a rise that looked down on the town. Below us, we saw the spires of the old gothic church where we were married. We could hear faint strains of organ music rising up from the church as someone practiced.

We stood there for a while listening to the sounds of nature and man. Elke finally nodded and I removed the top from the urn and handed it to her. She tilted it and the ashes of baby Lucy were caught in a downdraft and pulled away over the village, slowly dispersing and spreading out into a transparent cloud, reaching as far as the *Marktplatz*. Some of the ashes settled on the church, the City Hall and even the building where Elke's mother lived.

Elke took a last look at the village she had lived in all her life. She cried as we got back into the car and drove down to see her mother again.

We had coffee and cake and talked about Else coming to America to visit us once we settled down. She smiled all the while, hiding the pain of losing her daughter as well as her granddaughter. Suddenly, I realized what a strong person she really was. Her husband had died in a horrible war, and now a stranger was stealing away her only child. I was, in some ways, putting an end to her life. At that moment I felt like crying. She must have sensed my inner turmoil and patted me on the arm, smiling.

"It will be okay, John. It will be just fine," she said. She turned to Elke. "You must go and be a good wife to John. He will take good care of you, won't you, John?"

"Yes," I said. "I promise."

Else got an old photo album from a closet and handed it to me. "This is Elke's family history. It goes far back. You must keep it now, John."

"I'll take good care of it, *Mutti*."

I stood up and hugged and kissed Elke's mother. "Goodbye, *Mutti*," I said, using the familiar German word for mother.

"God-bless you, John," Else said. Her chin trembled.

"I'll wait in the car," I said.

I went downstairs and got into the car. Twenty minutes later Elke came down, crying. As we drove away, she waved at her mother who was standing in the doorway, just like the first time I had seen her. In a few seconds the road turned left and she was gone.

A week later we were on the S.S. United States steamer. Having a friend in the battalion travel section had paid off. It was not only a dream voyage for Elke but it helped her to heal. My little pixie strutted around the deck with the best of them. Of course, me being in uniform helped, too. People held the uniform in high regard and treated us like royalty.

On the morning that we cruised slowly into New York Harbor, everyone went up on deck to see the Statue of Liberty. We went early to get a good place at the rail. At first it was foggy but that soon cleared and Elke, at last, got her first live glimpse of the Statue of Liberty. She jumped up and down like a little girl and clapped her hands.

"Oh, Jawn! Look at her! Isn't she beautiful?" she said, pointing. "And she is green!" I laughed along with her.

Three hours later we were on American soil and on our way to the bus station for a trip to my next assignment at Fort Devens, Massachusetts.

One thing about the Army during that period was that it gave you had very little time to get bored. Elke loved to travel and yearned to see all the wonders of America. So, the

Army was a good fit for her. But as for me, I wanted to get back into civilian life and settle down in one place. My beloved angel, however, wanted me to stay in the service and I agreed to do that. I knew she was also hoping that in a few years we would be sent back to Germany.

But that was not to be. After three quickly passing years at Fort Devens we were sent to Camp Drum, New York. That lasted two years. After that, it was a year at Fort Meade, Maryland and on to Aberdeen Proving Grounds for two years.

In between all that moving around the country, Elke got her citizenship. I bought her a lot of nice clothes, and we took leave time to go on a cruise to Mexico and Puerto Rico. Also, I got two more promotions, ending up a Sergeant First Class. Elke was having the time of her life and so was I.

Then things quickly turned for the worst. I was given orders to report to the Defense Language Institute in California for a one-year course in Thai.

I was almost finished with training at the Language School in Monterey when my brother wrote me that my parents had died in a car accident. I was devastated and rushed home for the funeral. Returning to school, I finished up the year and was given my orders for Thailand. It was another one year tour. The worst part was, no spouses or dependents were allowed.

After talking it over, Elke and I agreed that we should buy a house. She would have access to our bank accounts and a car to drive around in. I would return in a year, serve out the rest of my re-enlistment time and retire from the army. We would go to Germany and spend some time with her mother and go on a second honeymoon to Spain. Elke was very happy with this plan.

We found a small, fully furnished house near the quaint little town of Cornwall-on-the-Hudson, thirty miles north of New York City. It was fully furnished and had a pool. Elke fell in love with it right away and we bought it with cold cash from my CDs and bonds. Money was no problem as my brother was willing and anxious to buy out my portion of the paper box factory owned by my family. My share was worth a third of a million dollars. I also had a sound stock portfolio.

After a sad goodbye, I left for Thailand where I spent a year in a stilt house on the Mae Kong River with a captain and a master sergeant, advising the Thai Army on S-3 type operations. Isolated most of the time, by the end of the tour I was practically an alcoholic. The heat and the humidity during the monsoon season were suffocating. It rained for weeks and there was nothing to do except play cards and drink. The only bright spot was writing to and receiving letters from Elke. I couldn't wait to get home again.

The final cut came at the end of the Thailand tour when I was given another set of orders to take a one month leave and then ship out again, this time to Vietnam. Then and there, I decided I'd had enough of being in the service. When and if I survived Vietnam, I would not re-enlist. After twenty years, I would end my Army career. It had been a wild ride and one that I had enjoyed, but it was time to call it quits. The army had given me a lot and I was grateful. Because of it I had met the sweetest, the most beautiful girl in the world, and that had made it all worthwhile. It was time to pack it in.

I finally made it home from Thailand to Elke. All I wanted was just to see her and touch her once more. It felt like a gift from God, a miracle, and it was like a second honeymoon. I held her in my arms for a long, long time, afraid to tell her that I would be shipping out again in another month. But I had to let her know and I did. I held her close and told her the awful news. I felt her flinch, then relax in my arms. Her heart was beating fast.

"Jawn," she whispered in my ear, "I love you and I always will."

We spent a glorious month together. It was as if we had just gotten married. We traveled and ate out and shopped. We talked about Germany, how we met, the good times we had with Frieda and Larsen. The trip to Spain and our first bullfight. She and her mother wrote each other regularly. I was happy because my angel was happy.

But it all ended too soon, and I left her crying at the airport as I boarded a plane for Los Angeles.

I spent two weeks at a processing depot at Fort Ord, California. After that it was a trip to Saigon and finally to a unit with the First Air Cavalry in central Vietnam. Whereas Korea had been a cold, dry, barren country, Vietnam was dense, warm and tropical. Whereas Korea had been a trench war, Vietnam was a search-and-destroy war where we sought out the North Vietnamese.

But they, just as often came, for us, too.

War Zone

My slow and easy days in the Army were over. This time I was transferred to an infantry unit positioned in the thick of things. Our unit had staked out a little pocket of earth in the middle of a rice paddy called a landing zone. The mission was to confront and do battle with Viet Cong fighters from the north.

Instead of a safe, cozy job behind a desk at Battalion Operations, I was now a platoon sergeant on a landing zone called LZ-Zebra. If you placed two football fields side by side, that would be about how large the area was. Around it, on all sides, were nothing but rice paddies and jungle. Our main contact with Battalion was by radio. The only reason I could think of for us being there was to attract the Viet Cong, which happened more often than we would have liked. All we could do was defend ourselves with our 60mm mortar, a 30-caliber machine gun, a few Claymore mines, some hand grenades and our M16 rifles. Of course, we could radio back to base for heavy artillery support if the situation got that bad. But the only way on or off the landing zone was on a helicopter or Caribou, a vintage WWII short takeoff and landing airplane.

The Viet Cong were brave, fierce soldiers who did not hesitate to bring the fight to us. While they were fighting a war of liberation, it seemed like we were fighting a war of occupation. We were strangers in a strange land. Yet, I never felt that they hated us personally. The whole mess felt more like a love-hate relationship than a war to the death over principles. Both sides took casualties each time we fought. Luckily, I was able to get our wounded out by chopper. But there were times when things got pretty rough and confused.

Sometimes personnel trained in special jungle warfare were flown in. They arrived in camouflage uniforms, with their faces painted to blend in with the jungle. They would go through a safe lane in our minefield and stay in the jungle for weeks at a time. Their job was to seek out and destroy Viet Cong leaders. Some never made it back.

The one day we looked forward to the most was when mail was brought in by chopper. Elke and I wrote to each other often. Her letters kept me going and I would have gone insane without them. Every two months we would get a rest and recuperation visit to a health spa in Saigon. There was a phone center there and I would call Elke. We would talk, and the sound of her voice kept me going through the horrible muck of war.

About a month before the end of my tour, my luck ran out. On that particular day we got hit by a larger than usual Viet Cong attack. It was instant chaos. A fierce firefight went on for hours and we began to take overwhelming casualties. Then it happened. I got hit in the side, just below the rib cage, with an AK-47 round. It passed through me, and hit the solder behind me in the heart, killing him instantly. I kept on firing into the Viet Cong until I collapsed and fell unconscious. Hours later, I awoke in a hospital in Saigon. I had lost a tremendous amount of blood.

The attack was beaten back by calling in heavy artillery and sending in reinforcements from the 1st Cavalry Division. Out of twenty-five men, I was one of ten found just barely alive. We were flown out by helicopter. Later I learned the LZ had been retaken. It had not been an easy task and cost many lives on both sides.

The doctors at the hospital in Saigon told me that I had come close to dying. The bullet had clipped my liver, damaging it. It had also touched an artery, but just barely. It was nip and tuck for a week but by some miracle I found the inner strength I needed to heal and keep on living. In my delirium, I thought Elke was by my side, holding my hand, speaking to me and smiling down at me.

Also, during those first days, while close to death, I was having a recurring nightmare. It wasn't quite clear enough to make out because I was burning up with fever. I think a large, white sheet, or something like a sheet, was chasing me but my legs would not move. The sheet closed over my face and smothered me so I couldn't breathe. All the time I had the feeling of an impending personal disaster. The dream came repeatedly, until my fever passed.

It was while I was in the recuperation ward that a young Captain came in to see me. He was holding a white envelope in his hand. When I saw it, my body gave an involuntary jerk. Just the sight of it made my heart pound. I must have turned pale.

"Should I call a nurse, Sergeant?" he asked.

"No, sir," I said. I felt nauseous but fought it back.

The Captain looked uncomfortable. He stared at the envelope a moment, not knowing what to say.

I spoke first. "My wife?"

He nodded and handed me the white envelope.

"The details are in there," he said. "I'm sorry for your losses."

"Losses, sir?" I asked.

"It's all in there," he said again. He handed me a card. "If you need anything, Sergeant, you can contact me there." He pointed at the card and left.

I was afraid to open the envelope. I turned it around in my hand a few times, and then held it up to see who had sent it. It was addressed to me, but had the return address of the hospital near our home. Elke's doctor practiced there. It was where she got her yearly physical examination.

I slowly opened it. My head was reeling and pounding as I read it. It was from her doctor. He regretted to inform me that Elke had passed away while giving birth. The baby was stillborn. I was to contact him as soon as possible as to what to do with the deceased.

There was another letter in it, one Elke had written just before she died in the delivery room, addressed to me.

Darling, please forgive me, but when you came home on leave from Thailand and told me you were going to Vietnam soon, I panicked, and so, when we made love, I didn't take precautions as I usually do. I wanted to have a little John so he could grow up big and brave and strong like his father in case you never came back to me. Oh, John, I love you so much. I will always love you. I have loved you in life and I shall love you in death. You will always know and feel that love, my darling. Please come back to me, my love I pray for your safety. Yours forever and ever, your wife, Elke.

I was numb with pain. I howled like a wounded animal and the nurses came and shoved a needle in me to sedate me. I fought against it and they gave me a second shot. That one put me under. I don't remember much about what went on for about a week after that. When I was stabilized, I telephoned the hospital and spoke to the doctor. I asked him to have Elke and the baby cremated. I would be coming home to get the remains.

About two weeks after I left Saigon, it fell to the Viet Cong. Adding to my sorrow was the thought of all the fine soldiers I had served with who never made it back. I thanked God for the guardian angel who had seen me through. Perhaps it was the same one who had guided me to Elke years ago.

Farewell

With less than a year left in the Army, I was assigned to Fort Devens, with a thirty day leave starting immediately. I left Saigon, flew to Los Angeles and then on to New York. I caught a trunk flight to Stewart Airfield and then took a taxi home.

Walking into the living room, I stopped and listened, expecting to feel my beloved angel come rushing into my arms. I wanted to hear her sweet voice saying, "Welcome home, Jawn," but there was only the silence of an empty house and the ticking of the clock in the kitchen.

I set my duffel bag down and went slowly up to the bedroom. Walking into the big closet, I put the light on and stared at the dresses and pairs of shoes that Elke once wore. Her scent was still there. Knowing it would eventually fade away, I inhaled it deeply and wept like a baby. After a while, I went down to the great room and got the vodka bottle. I took it into the kitchen, intending to get drunk, but poured it down the sink. I was completely exhausted from the thousands of miles of traveling, so I walked upstairs, undressed and got into bed. I could smell the scent of her favorite perfume on the pillow and it set me off to crying again.

A long while later, I fell asleep. When I woke up, it was evening and I was hungry. I showered, dressed in civilian clothes, got in the car and drove around for hours.

The next day I got up early and drove to the hospital to see Elke's doctor. He was very understanding and had taken care of the cremation part for me. I settled all accounts and drove to the funeral parlor that had taken care of the cremations. I paid the bill and took the urns holding Elke's and the baby's ashes.

When I got back home I combined them in a single urn. That evening I put the urn and some civilian clothes into a suitcase, then put the suitcase in the trunk of the car. The next morning, after a quick breakfast, I got back into uniform, locked the house, got in the car and headed for Dover Air Base, in Delaware. I arrived late at night, parked on the base and took a room at the guesthouse.

I had a two day wait, but I finally got a space available ride on a jumbo cargo plane to Ramstein Air Base. I was just another army sergeant visiting old friends in Germany. I was so tired I slept most of the way over.

Once at Ramstein, I changed into civilian clothing and rented a car. The day was still young so I drove to the *Kaserne* outside of Hanau, hoping my old unit was there. It was gone. The Americans had moved somewhere else and a German engineering contracting firm had moved in. The barracks room where Larsen and I had slept had been converted into a series of cubicles for busy clerks.

I drove into Hanau again and parked near a *bratwurst* and beer vendor. I ate there, rested for a while, then drove north to Meerholz. I drove the same road that Larsen and I had traveled hundreds of times. It was a nice, sunny summer's day, a good day for a drive in the country.

I arrived at Meerholz in the afternoon and parked in front of the teacher's house where the party had taken place. For some reason, it appeared sad and lonely. Its paint was peeling and it looked empty and neglected. Time and the elements had not been kind to it. I could feel it because I felt that way, too. I guess I had expected to see German high school kids running in and out, laughing and singing, like that time so long ago when I had met Elke. But there was no one, nothing except a "For Sale" sign out front.

For a fleeting moment, I thought I heard laughter inside, but it could have only been the wind. I knocked on the door and someone called for me to come in. Entering the hallway, I saw an elderly woman sitting behind a small desk near the entrance.

"Good afternoon," I said.

"Oh, American! You're not interested in buying this house, are you?" she asked, in English, smiling.

"No," I said. "I was here once, many years ago, with a friend." Then I added, "I'm just passing through so I thought I would stop by and look around." I had trouble speaking. I was afraid I was going to break down and cry.

She stared at me sympathetically and smiled. "Old memories, yes?"

"Yes," I said.

"I know how that is. Please look around, if you wish. Take all the time you need."

"Thank you, thanks very much."

Walking slowly past her desk, I went through the open door into the kitchen. The place where the food and drink had been, was now empty. I looked for the spot where I had sat down in the cookie dough, laughing inwardly as I re-imagined it happening. There were no stools there now. The tables, chairs and even the big stove were gone. The laundry room was empty, too.

I stood awhile looking around then retraced my steps back into the hall and walked upstairs to the book room. On the way up, I imagined I could hear the shouts and laughter of the young German kids echoing faintly up above.

I also thought I heard voices. "This is Elke," Frieda was saying.

"Oh, hello, Jawn," a sweet, lyrical voice said. "Why are you staring at me, Jawn?" It was a sweet memory echoing from the past.

Standing alone on the second floor landing, I stared into the book room. The bookshelves were now empty as was the spot where the rickety old chair had been, where Elke had plopped down on my lap that fateful day.

"Don't let me fall, Jawn!" A pause: "Would you cry for me if you loved me and I was dying, Jawn?"

I heard my own voice answering, "You're not planning to die soon, are you…" and then I added three more words to the sentence, "…my beloved angel?"

I held the scene of us in my mind, listening to the sweet sound of her musical laughter. It felt good to be there. I could feel her presence even in the emptiness. It would always be there. I wanted to stay in that place forever, listening to the sounds of those precious moments from the past.

I stood there alone for a long time, listening to those mellifluous, spectral echoes, listening until they stopped when a noise downstairs interrupted them. The only thing that remained after that were the subdued sounds of the old house creaking on its ancient foundation. I finally forced myself to go downstairs.

"Thank you," I said to the woman.

She stared at me. "Are you alright?" I nodded and left.

Outside I took one last look at the house. It now cast a long, cold, black shadow on the road. I walked reluctantly to the car and got in, feeling as if I were leaving a part of my life behind me, a part I would gladly relive again and again.

I drove north towards Gelnhausen to see Elke's mother. I arrived by mid-evening and went up to her flat. I knocked on the door but when no one answered I went across the hall to knock there. A woman came out.

"Yes?"

"I've come to see Else Wester. Is she home?"

She looked sadly at me, shook her head and replied in English, "I guess you don't know. She died last week."

I suddenly felt cold and all alone. All I could do was repeat what she had said, "She died last week?"

"Yes, she died last week."

"What happened, do you know?"

The woman slowly brought her hand up, patted her chest and said, "Yes. Her heart." She stared at me again as if trying to place my face. "Are you a friend?"

"I'm her son-in-law," I replied, then thanked her and started to leave.

'Oh, yes," she said. "I remember. Many, many years ago."

"Yes," I replied.

"And, Elke? She is well?"

"She has passed away," I replied, choking up.

"I am so very sorry. Would you like coffee?"

"No, but thank you very much".

I went downstairs and walked across the plaza to a flower shop, bought a small bouquet, then drove to the edge of town and put the flowers in front of the plain grave marker with Elke's mother's name on it. It was next to the gravestone of Elke's father. I stayed a while and went back to the car, sitting for a long time, feeling completely exhausted.

I drove up to the hill above the town where Elke and I had gone to release baby Lucy's ashes. I got the urn from the car, walked over to where Elke and I had last stood, and looked down on the village. I was the only one there at that hour, yet somehow, I didn't feel alone. It was as if Elke was standing right there beside me.

"Would you cry for me, Jawn, if you loved me?" a voice seemed to whisper close by.

It could only have been the wind, but I answered, "Yes, my darling, yes!"

I released the ashes. They floated out and down towards the village. It was a long time before the last of them had disappeared. I stood there sobbing. "Yes, my darling, yes, I will cry for you!"

And I cried for a long time. After a while, I got in the car and drove back to Ramstein.

I wanted to return to our house as quickly as possible because I felt her spirit would be there waiting for me. It would always be there and I wanted to be there too, close to her. In that sense, she was still alive within me. It was something I felt, but couldn't explain. Somehow, I could feel her presence, her energy.

I spent the rest of my leave at home and then reported to my new unit at Fort Devens. Eleven months later, I ended my career in the military and went to live the life of a retired soldier. The house was a safe haven where I could exist with my precious memories in quiet solitude, with those sweet reveries that I never wanted to fade away.

I guess I was purposely turning myself into some sort of a recluse. There were times when I felt sad and times when I felt happy. Much of my attention was devoted to Elke's garden. I often found myself speaking to my beloved angel as I tended to the wisteria. She had planted it by the side of the house when we first moved in. Whenever its sweet smelling, purplish flowers bloomed, it reminded me of her.

I often looked at those dresses and shoes of hers that I kept in the bedroom closet, thinking how lovely she had looked in them. Finally, I decided to give them to charity. All but one special black dress that I kept because Elke had looked so gorgeous and elegant in it. Every so often, down through the years, I would be tempted to give it away but could not bring myself to do it. I hung onto it for over ten years, until I finally did let it go.

Reveries

She often came to me in my reveries. I liked and welcomed that. As I worked in the little flower garden that was once hers, Elke would appear in my mind's eye and talk to me. Of course, there were other times, too, like whenever I drank too much. During those times, I cried a lot and felt very sad. I even thought about ending my life.

It was on one of those days, when my brain was half-soaked in gin, that I convinced myself that by ending my life here on earth, all my sorrow would go away. I would be with Elke in our own little paradise for eternity. I nourished that fantasy many times in the past. One night, I decided to act on it.

Grabbing a bottle of gin from the cabinet in the living room, I got the sharpest knife from the kitchen drawer and carried them upstairs to the master bedroom. Once there, I filled the bathtub full of hot water, undressed and lay down in it. The water was very soothing. I lay back and closed my eyes, waiting for the right moment to act. I felt comfortable and relaxed in that little cocoon of warmth, drinking and nodding off and waking up again. Each time I woke up, I drank some more gin. Eventually, I decided I was drunk enough to do the fateful deed.

Just as I was about cut my wrist, I thought I heard Elke's voice saying to me, "What about our story, Jawn?"

In my inebriated condition, I heard myself answering, "What story, my love?"

"Everybody has a story, Jawn. Even Frieda and Larsen had a story, as sad as it was."

"Yes, you're right, my love. They did have a story. I never thought about that, my angel."

"Well, you should have, Jawn," she seemed to say. "When you're dead our story will die with you and that would just be awful."

"But, what should I do, my love?"

"Jawn, don't be stupid. You know very well what to do. Must I push you down into the cookie dough again?"

I chuckled. "The cookie dough? Now that would make a good story, wouldn't it, darling?"

"Yes, I think it would, Jawn. I always thought it would," Then, after a short pause, I heard her say, "Well, are you going to do it or not?"

"Do what, my dear?"

"Write our story, my love."

"Now? Right now?"

"Of course, Jawn. Get up and go down to the study and get it started. There will never be a better time, you know!"

Suddenly the tub water felt ice cold and I realized I was shivering. The whole cutting of the wrist thing didn't seem like such a good idea anymore.

Hungry and shivering, I staggered out of the tub and struggled into my robe. It took me a while to make my way safely down to the kitchen without breaking a leg, but once there, I made a pot of strong, black coffee. The first thing I did was drink a full cup. After that, I built a Dagwood Bumstead sandwich and carried it and a cup of coffee into the den. Placing them on the desk, I got a large legal pad and a pencil from a drawer and commenced writing. As I wrote, I took bites of the sandwich and sips of the coffee. My intentions were to write my thoughts down now and type them later. I started slow, unsure of myself, but began to write very fast as memories came gushing from the past.

I could hear my little pixie giggling over my shoulder. "And don't forget the cookie dough, Jawn! Don't forget the cookie dough! That's the best part."

"The cookie dough? Oh, yes, the cookie dough! No, I won't forget that, my darling," I said, "I could never, ever forget the cookie dough, my love!" Then I said, "You know, it was nasty of you to do that to me, darling. Don't you think so?"

"Yes, but the look on your face was worth it, Jawn."

"I'm sure it was, my love."

I chuckled to myself and kept on writing. I could smell the sweet perfume of the wisteria blooms outside the window. It reminded me of the scent of Elke's hair.

The End

About the Author

R. Annan is a well-traveled author with many interests. As a career serviceman, he served in Korea and Vietnam. He also completed a one-year course at the Defense Language Institute in Monterey, California, and graduated from the University of South Florida with a B.A. in Art and Art History. After taking a two-year course in screenwriting at the Hollywood Scriptwriting Institute, he established The Old Time Radio Club Time Machine as both a scriptwriter and an actor.

Other books by R. Annan:

Mr. Dobbs: A Christmas Ghost Story
The Ghost of Reginald Burton, Esquire
Vzor's Prisoner: A Sci-fi Novel
The Princess of Ovaar: A Sci-fi Fantasy
Gemma's Angel
Sen Loi
The Barnhart Intruder

Western books by R. Annan:

The Fight for The Lazy M
The Red Bandana
The Salvation of Trace Logan
Jack Cordell Westerns
Jesse Garnett Westerns